DISNEY · PIXAR
COCO

Adapted by
Adrian Molina

Illustrated by
Fabiola Garza

Designed by
Tony Fejeran

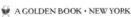 A GOLDEN BOOK · NEW YORK

Copyright © 2017 Disney Enterprises, Inc. and Pixar. All rights reserved. Published in the United States by Golden Books, an imprint of Random House Children's Books, a division of Penguin Random House LLC, 1745 Broadway, New York, NY 10019, and in Canada by Penguin Random House Canada Limited, Toronto, in conjunction with Disney Enterprises, Inc. Golden Books, A Golden Book, A Little Golden Book, the G colophon, and the distinctive gold spine are registered trademarks of Penguin Random House LLC.

randomhousekids.com

ISBN 978-0-7364-3800-1 (trade) — ISBN 978-0-7364-3801-8 (ebook)

Printed in the United States of America

10 9 8 7 6 5 4 3 2 1

In the **small** town of Santa Cecilia, there lived a boy named Miguel Rivera. His house was **full** of family, including his great-grandmother, Mamá Coco.

Every year on Día de los Muertos, the Day of the Dead, his family shared the **memories** of relatives who had passed on.

Miguel's abuelita would tell the story of his great-great-grandmother, Mamá Imelda, whose heart had been **broken** by her musician husband. Because of him, there was one rule in the Rivera household: **NO MUSIC!**

But Miguel LOVED music. In his secret hideout, he
learned to play guitar by watching videos of his favorite
musician, Ernesto de la Cruz.

Inspired, Miguel snuck out of the house one night with
his dog, Dante, to perform in a local talent show.

But on the way out, Dante **jumped**
onto the family ofrenda, or altar. Mamá
Imelda's photo **tumbled** down with a

crash!

Papá!

That was when Miguel made a **discovery.**
Mamá Imelda's husband was holding a guitar—
and it looked very familiar!

"Mamá Coco's papá was **Ernesto de la Cruz!**" Miguel cried. "I'm going to be a **musician!**"

But because of their family rule, his abuelita took his guitar and destroyed it.

SMASH!

Miguel ran as FAST as he could to Ernesto's tomb, where the musician's famous guitar still hung. Taking it off the wall, he said, "Please don't be mad. I need this to be a musician like you!" And he gave the legend's guitar a strum.

All of a sudden, Miguel noticed all the SKELETONS around him! They had followed the path of marigold petals to visit their living relatives for Día de los Muertos.

To return to the Land of the Living,
Miguel would need a **blessing** from one
of his dead family members. So he and
Dante crossed the Marigold Bridge into
the **Land of the Dead**.

Miguel found Mamá Imelda, but she said she wouldn't give him her blessing if he wanted to be a **musician**. Miguel had to find another way.

So he teamed up with a skeleton named **Hector**, who said he knew Ernesto de la Cruz.

With some shoe polish, Hector made Miguel look like a **skeleton**.

They traveled all over looking for Ernesto. They even performed together in a **talent show**!

But Miguel was running out of time. If he didn't get Ernesto's blessing soon, he'd turn into a **REAL** skeleton and never get home!

So he **ditched** Hector to find his great-great-grandpa on his own.

Miguel snuck into Ernesto's fiesta at the **tippy-top** of a tall tower. But the place was so crowded, he couldn't get to Ernesto.

So Miguel belted out a song! Everyone watched as he sang . . . and **fell** into Ernesto's pool.

Splash!

The skeletons saw that he was **a living boy.**

Ernesto was **overjoyed**
to meet Miguel!

"I have a
**great-
great-
grandson!**"

But then Hector appeared,
and as the two men argued,
Miguel learned the **dark truth.**

His great-great-grandpa
had **poisoned** Hector and
stolen his songs to become
famous.

Miguel was shocked to see Ernesto's
face turn cold. Ernesto explained that he
couldn't risk letting the world know the
truth. Then he threw Miguel and Hector

down,

down,

down

into a dark pit.

Hector told Miguel that all the songs he'd written were for his **family**. And there was a special **lullaby**, "Remember Me." He always sang it for his daughter, Coco.

Miguel thought of Mamá Imelda's photo and the unidentified man. "It's you! Hector, YOU are my great-great-grandpa!"

Suddenly, Mamá Imelda and Dante came to their **rescue**.

But Hector began to **disappear**. His daughter was starting to **forget** him.

Mamá Imelda and Hector sent Miguel **home** with their blessing.

Back in the Land of the Living,
Miguel rushed to Mamá Coco. He sang
"Remember Me" to remind her of her
papá. She usually didn't talk much,
so Miguel was thrilled when she
began to sing along!

Mamá Coco kept her **papá's** memory alive by sharing stories of him with her relatives. At last, the Riveras realized that music could bring them closer together.

And now Miguel knew he could follow his dream and become a musician—with his family's **support**.